Best Frien...
Special Frie...

For Marc and Richard

ORCHARD BOOKS
96 Leonard Street, London EC2A 4XD
Orchard Books Australia
32/45-51 Huntley Street, Alexandria, NSW 2015
ISBN 1 84121 156 7 (hardback)
ISBN 1 84121 288 1 (paperback)
First published in Great Britain in 2002
First paperback publication in 2003
Text and Illustrations © Susan Rollings 2002
The right of Susan Rollings to be identified as the author and illustrator
of this work has been asserted by her in accordance with the
Copyright, Designs and Patents Act, 1988.
A CIP catalogue record for this book is available from the British Library.
(hardback) 10 9 8 7 6 5 4 3 2 1
(paperback) 10 9 8 7 6 5 4 3 2 1
Printed in Singapore

Best Friends Special Friends

Susan Rollings

ORCHARD BOOKS

those who
wake you up friends.

Busy friends,
nosy friends

time to go to
school friends.

Slow friends,
fast friends

racing round the
playground friends.

Tall friends,
small friends

some are very
clever friends.

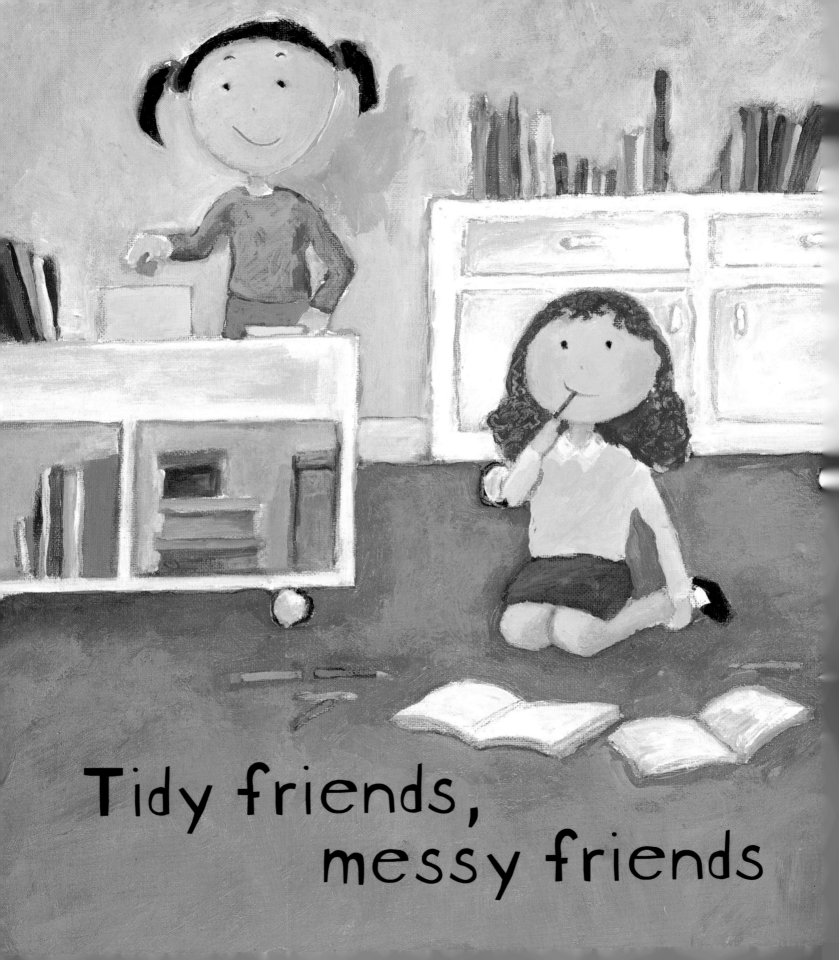

Tidy friends,
messy friends

kind and very
         helpful friends.

definitely NOT
my friend!

Wet friends,
cheeky friends

listening to the
story friends.

Sad friends,
happy friends

skipping out at
home time friends.

Quiet friends,
 noisy friends

Playing in the Park friends.

Furry friends,
    feathered friends

quacking, squeaking,
hungry friends.

Old friends,
new friends

I really have
a LOT of friends.

My friends,
special friends

surprise, surprise,
it's ALL my friends!